THE ADVENTURES OF PuppyCat

By Mitchell Kriegman

Illustrated by Deborah Barrett

Based on a concept by Deborah Barrett

A BANTAM LITTLE ROOSTER BOOK
NEW YORK · TORONTO · LONDON · SYDNEY · AUCKLAND

D0386232

In Kibbletown the dogs are mean, and the cats are scared. Dog City, some call it, where the only way to avoid being cornered by a snarling pack of canines is to get up early and be ready to run like blazes.

Tabby awoke, rubbing his eyes and straightening his whiskers. Living on the edge of Kibbletown was dangerous, but it was the only home Tabby had ever known. Life for cats was easier in Tunaville, just across the tracks. There the cats were still asleep, dreaming of catnip, warm milk, and slow mice.

Tabby stepped into the yard to greet the morning. But before he could rub the sleep from his eyes, he heard a raucous barking.

OWOWOWOW! Winfreed, the neighborhood hound, jumped out from behind a row of tall bushes. Tabby dashed across the sidewalk. He leapt over the mailbox. He twisted around the corner. Another escape!

Winfreed's barking had put all the other dogs in the neighborhood on Cat Alert. So Tabby slinked cautiously past the house where the dalmatians lived. The dalmatian twins, Tick and Tack, were fast and mean. *YAPYAPYAP!* The twins came ripping toward

him from around the porch! Tabby
cursed himself for being caught off guard.
He zoomed toward the alley that led to his
house. There was Winfreed again, smiling,
and waiting for him! *YAPYAPYAP!* Tabby heard
Tick and Tack yelping and leaping behind him.

"How did they get here so fast?" he panted.
He clawed his way up the rickety wooden
fence. *OWOWOWOW!* There
were racing dogs,
barking snouts, scraping
paws, and flying fur
everywhere! Quickly,
he zigged instead of
zagged and skidded
right through the

back door of his house, safe at last from the dogs of Kibbletown.

"What a mess!" Tabby cried. His fur stuck out in every direction. His paws were shaking. "I can't go on like this!" he said.

After a soothing glass of milk, he smoothed his ruffled fur with his tongue. Then he crawled back to bed and tucked himself in. "What do they have against me?" he wondered. Suddenly, out of nowhere, a terrifying shadow of a huge dog stretched across the bedroom wall. *A dog inside the house? Unthinkable!*

On the very tips of his padded paws, Tabby backed slowly, inch by inch, toward the door. But the farther he moved, the bigger the shadow became. It was the biggest dog ever. Tabby dropped the blanket and started through the door. But then— the shadow vanished.

"What's going on here?" he asked. Unwrinkling his whiskers, Tabby picked up the blanket and wrapped himself in it again. Mysteriously the shadow reappeared. When he dropped the blanket, the shadow vanished once more. There wasn't a dog in the house at all. It was a shadow of Tabby wrapped in his own blanket!

"Hey cat!" a wiry voice called. "What are you afraid of? You've got nine lives." Tabby hissed. He knew that squeaky voice. It was Zagreus, Zag for short, the mouse of the house. Tabby was in no mood for wisecracks. He was thinking very hard, so hard that he began pacing around the room. Zag watched Tabby circle, deep in thought.

"I've got it!" he said finally.

"Got what?" asked the mouse. But without another word, Tabby began scratching out all sorts of drawings. Zag looked on as he sketched spitzes, scamps, spaniels, and Saint Bernards.

He drew poodles, Pekingese, Pomeranians, and pugs. Then Tabby turned the house upside-down, snatching up shabby old clothes, tattered pieces of rugs, torn towels, and any little piece of fabric he could lay his paws on. His tail curled with delight when he discovered a frayed fur coat.

"I'll never be chased by dogs again!" he exclaimed.

All day and into the night Tabby cut and sewed. "This cat must have fur balls for brains," Zag declared, mystified by all the activity. But he helped where he could, threading needles and sewing in the places that Tabby couldn't reach with his paws.

By night's end the cat stood proudly before the mirror. Zag looked on in disbelief. "That's the strangest outfit I've ever seen. What is it?"

"A dog suit!" Tabby answered, turning to examine the stitching on his new floppy dog ears. He was the funniest looking canine ever, not a fancy dachshund or Doberman, but a scruffy, rag-eared mutt.

"You're not just a tabby cat anymore," Zag remarked. "You're a...PuppyCat!" Tabby liked the sound of it.

The cat hardly slept that night. In his dreams, Winfreed, Tick and Tack, and every other dog in the neighborhood took turns chasing him. By morning he had curled and uncurled so many times in his sleep that his whiskers were tied in knots.

Zag was awakened by a most unpleasant sound. He found PuppyCat in the kitchen, trying to bark. "That bark wouldn't fool a dog catcher," Zag said as he climbed up onto the table.

PuppyCat took an angry swipe at the mouse. "You're no help!" he said.

He tried every kind of bark—*woofs, arfs, ruffs, yaps, yelps,* and *bowwows.* It seemed hopeless. But then he tried growling. *Grrr. Grrrr. Grrrrrrr. Grrrruuuuffff! Gruff! Gruff!* "That's it!" he croaked. "It's a purr-fect bark!"

PuppyCat practiced all morning. He learned to lower his voice, sit with his paws in the air, pant with his tongue hanging out, and wag his tail.

As the sun rose high over Old Bone Hill, PuppyCat zipped up his suit and walked out the front door. The time had come for him to put his plan into action. Zag watched from the window and waved good-bye.

That's when Puppycat turned and found himself nose to nose with Winfreed. But Winfreed only huffed, brushed herself off, and trotted away.

"It works!" PuppyCat exclaimed. He crossed the street, passing the dalmatian twins along the way. Tick and Tack walked right past him without a growl. PuppyCat could hardly believe it, the dog suit *was* a success.

Then he saw Beauford. PuppyCat's claws dug into the grass. He hoped the big growler would pass him by. But Beauford had already noticed him. He circled PuppyCat slowly, sniffing.

"Gruff, gruff," PuppyCat barked.

"You must be new around here," Beauford said in a voice that sounded like gravel. PuppyCat was too frightened to speak. "What's the matter?" Beauford asked. "Cat got your tongue?" PuppyCat choked on those words. The big dog patted him on the back with his heavy paw. "It's a joke, son, just a joke," he said, offering his paw in friendship.

"Why don't you let me show you around?" Beauford suggested. "I'm on my way to the Hound Dawg Club. They're putting on a dog show today." Beauford put his arm around PuppyCat. "I'll show you the secret entrance," he whispered.

With a wag of his tail, the old growler led PuppyCat down the street. PuppyCat wanted desperately to run up the nearest tree. He wished he had never thought of making a dog suit. But there was no turning back. Zag watched from the house shaking his head as the two disappeared. "This could be the end," Zag thought sadly.

Beauford led PuppyCat through the open bottom of an overturned garbage can that covered a hole in the fence. PuppyCat closed his eyes as they entered. When he opened them, he almost jumped out of his dog suit. There were dogs,

dogs, and more dogs! He was right in the middle of them, swept along by a river of snouts, tails, teeth, and paws!

There were dogs scratching fleas. Dogs sniffing each other. Dogs paw wrestling. Dogs playing cards. Just being in the same alley with all those dogs made PuppyCat's hair bristle. Then with a hush, the dog show began. But this was unlike any dog show PuppyCat had ever heard of.

This was a talent show. At center stage stood the host, Burt Barks. Behind him was a band that called themselves the Hound Dawg Five.

Everyone sang along as they played "You Ain't Nothing But a Hound Dawg!" Then, one by one, each dog in the audience took the stage and performed.

A bone-juggling bulldog
kept four bones in the air
at once. A fat basset
hound sang an aria from
a Poochini opera.

PuppyCat was being pushed toward the stage by two frolicking pups. He did everything he could to slip away. But he was next! As the pups pushed him backstage, PuppyCat heard Burt say, "And now I'm pleased to introduce a newcomer to Kibbletown!" That's when it happened. PuppyCat didn't see the nail at the backstage stairway. *R-r-r-r-rip.* The dog suit was torn away!

Tabby stood naked—a cat in front of a sea of dogs. The entire audience was silent. Tabby stared. The dogs stared back.

Then backstage he heard a tiny whisper. "Stall them," the familiar little voice said. "Do *something!*"

It was Zag, gnawing furiously on the snagged threads of the dog suit.

Every dog's eyes were focused on the stage. Tabby heard his own voice break the silence. "I would like to do my impression... of...of a cat. *Meow! Meow!*" he cried in his squeakiest, highest voice. The crowd howled with laughter. "And this is my impression of a cat taking a bath."

He licked his fur with dainty feline licks. PuppyCat pulled out all the stops. He arched his back and hissed. He curled his tail. The dogs cheered and burst into applause.

"Hurry up!" Zag called from offstage. The dog suit was free. Tabby made a quick bow, dashed from the stage, and jumped into the dog suit.

"Let's get out of here!" he said as Burt Barks called for an encore. They jumped over a pile of garbage cans and leapt onto the top of the tall fence. PuppyCat heard Burt and Beauford calling him.

Zag stopped suddenly. Looking to the ground far below, his mouse ears drooped. "I'll never make it!" he said.

"Hold on!" PuppyCat said. And grabbing the mouse, he sailed to the gravel path below. PuppyCat landed squarely on all four paws—a smooth landing any cat would have been proud of.

Back at home, PuppyCat unzipped the dog suit and collapsed into his chair. Zag paced the floor excitedly. "Did you see those dogs?" he asked. "That was the best impression of a cat by a cat...I mean, as a dog you're the best cat I've ever seen—what I mean is...what an adventure!"

"Wow! What a day!" PuppyCat said, feeling oddly pleased as he absentmindedly nipped at a flea. Then he sighed and fell into a silent snooze.